Aberdeenshire Library and Information Service

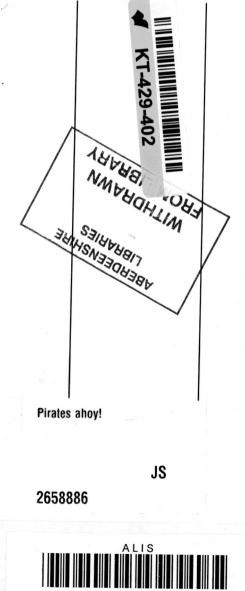

Pirates ahoy!

JS

Other books in the same series:

Bobby, Charlton and the Mountain

'An excellent story . . . the first-person voice of the narrator is so immediate, so animated.'

TES

Man of the Match

Shortlisted for the
Highland Children's Book Awards.

Selected by Chelsea Football Club as the nominated title in a reading scheme run in association with the National Literacy Trust.

Team Trouble

'Simple and unpretentious, this novel manages to convey the warmth and humour of family life.'

School Librarian

Pirates Ahoy!

SOPHIE SMILEY

Illustrated by
MICHAEL FOREMAN

Andersen Press
London

First published in Great Britain in 2009
by Andersen Press Limited,
20 Vauxhall Bridge Road, London SW1V 2SA
www.andersenpress.co.uk

Text © Sophie Smiley, 2009
Illustration © Michael Foreman, 2009

British Library Cataloguing in Publication Data available.
ISBN 978 184 270 882 8

Printed in the UK by CPI Bookmarque, Croydon, CR0 4TD

To Dean and Leah Martin
and
Ciara-Marie and Anja Quarmby.

Chapter 1

'Bring back some treasure!'
Gran called, as we set off for
the seaside.

'Yo ho ho and a bottle of rum,'
Gramps waved.

'Yo ho ho and a bottle of bum!'
Bobby sang as we drove along. He
pulled a hat over one eye and
went, 'Ahr, ahr, pieces of eight.'

'Why are pirates called pirates?'
Dad asked.

'Because they aaAHRR!' said
Bobby.

'What does a pirate say when
you ask him if he knows any pirate
jokes?' Dad continued.

'AHRRR you kidding me?!'

'What does a pirate call his
mum?' Dad was on a roll.

'MothAHRRR, mothAHRR,'
said Bobby.

'Any more of that and I'll make
you walk the plank,' Mum said,
looking up from the football pages,
'and I'll send your DVD down to
Davy Jones.'

You see Gran had given Bobby
a pirate film for his birthday. He
watched it over and over again.
Pirates were the only thing he

wanted to play nowadays. My family has always been football mad and we normally talk about goals and tackles, but as we began our holiday, it was all life on the ocean wave. That film had turned us from a five-a-side football team into a bunch of swashbuckling pirates!

Well, Dad and Bobby carried on. But I didn't join in. I'd had enough. It was all very well for Bobby to be a pirate hero, but I didn't want to play the silly heroine who needs rescuing. I've never been a girly-whirly kind of girl – even my name, Charlton, sounds like a boy's name. (We were called after my dad's World Cup hero, Bobby Charlton). I wished my youngest brother, Bobby, would stop being a pirate. I wanted him back – back defending his goal, not soppy damsels in distress!

Chapter 2

When we reached the caravan, I was surprised that Bobby didn't fight me for the top bunk. He disappeared while I arranged my football mags, put on my boots and grabbed a football. Outside, the camp site was quiet. That spooky silence you get before a penalty shoot-out; the scary kind of quiet that tells me Bobby's up to something. I searched the grass:

it was empty. Usually, the first thing Bobby does when he arrives anywhere is build a goal; today there were no goal posts and no sign of Bobby.

I ran to the cliff edge and peered over. My stomach lurched as I saw the rocks. I looked along the sand. Nothing. And not a sound.

Then, from behind me, came a muffled thud, thud, thud. I ran towards a huge oak tree. What was happening? I was almost at the tree when I got a shower of dirt in my face. I stopped dead. What had attacked me?

Clearing mud from my eyes, I heard a voice coming from the

tree. 'Pieces of eight, pieces of eight.'

I tiptoed forward, and peered round the trunk. There was Bobby, digging his way to Australia!

Dad appeared saying, 'Pirates bury their treasure in the sand – let's find the beach.'

But at that moment, my big brothers, Wembley and Striker, arrived on their bicycles. They'd left hours before us. My middle brother, Semi, and his girlfriend, Primrose, pedalled up behind them on a tandem. When they saw Bobby they started singing, 'Jumped aboard a pirate ship and the captain said to me . . . '

Bobby joined in, and we all scrambled down the cliff path.

'Football?' I asked when we reached the beach. I began marking out a pitch.

But Bobby wasn't interested in football. Or the sea. He'd spotted some gulls.

'Come on, come on,' he coaxed,

trying to get one of them
to sit on his shoulder
like a parrot. They
swooshed to
and fro ignoring
him, until Mum opened the picnic
basket. Once Bobby had a roll in
his hand, all the gulls
swooped. Bobby stared
as they snatched his
dinner. 'Burglars!' he shouted,
waving his fists at them. Then he
flapped his arms and yelled, 'Go
away, bad birds!'

One of them
hovered. A large,
white poo
splattered onto
Bobby's head.

'Ugh – yucky, yuk yuk.'

At least that'll put him off seagulls, I thought, now we can play football.

'Hey, Bobs,' I said, 'the sand is really soft – great for goalies – look,' and I dived, whoomph, flat out. Bobby looked up. He's the best goalie in his school. (He goes to a special school 'cos he's got Down's syndrome. He has a bigger football field than mine, but Mum says my school's special too – just different.)

I kicked the ball towards him but he hardly noticed as it rolled past.

'Dig for treasure,' he said, picking up a spade and flinging sand in all directions.

Mum spat a sandy sandwich from her mouth, peeped her whistle, flashed a yellow card and said, 'No treasure hunting near the food!'

Mum's the ref in our house, and no one messes about when she gets out a yellow card. Bobby moved further down the beach – he didn't wait for the red one!

He started digging a new hole. It grew deeper and deeper.

The big boys and Primrose went swimming. I can swim, but I've hated water ever since Kevin Joggs pushed me in the deep end. The sea is even worse than the pool – full of slimy jellyfish and nippy crabs.

I asked Dad for a game of football, but he said he was going for ice cream. Mum usually gives me header practice, but today all she wanted was a snooze.

I kicked a ball crossly against the sea wall. A drink's can flew from Bobby's hole. A flip-flop.

Then a shampoo bottle looped out, sailed over and bopped me on the head. I'd had enough. Sometimes my temper bursts like a volcano. 'That's another yellow card,' I stormed. 'Mum, show him the red, he's . . . '

Bobby scrambled out of the hole and said, 'Not doing anything—'

'There's Dad with the ice creams,' Mum tried to distract us.

Dad waved the cornets, and shouted, 'Ahoy there, me hearties!'

He was nearly at Bobby's treasure hole.

'Look out, Dad!' I yelled.

Too late. Dad disappeared.

We all stared.

Slowly, an upside-down ice-cream cone rose from the sand. It was attached to Dad's head. Raspberry topping trickled down his face like blood.

We gasped.

Then a spooky voice boomed, 'Fifteen men on a dead man's chest – yo ho ho and a bottle of rum!' He staggered towards us, lumbering around like a skeleton pirate.

When everyone had finished giggling, I tried again. 'Football?'

'Ooh, not with my Long John Silver leg.' Dad pretended to hobble.

'Football, pleeease?' I begged.

'Pirates,' Bobby said stubbornly.

The deckchair flapped, and I had an idea. Planting the chair next to his treasure hole, I said, 'That can be your pirate ship, Bobby.'

The chair seat billowed like a real sail.

'You'll have to defend it, 'cos my ship's coming. Watch out – cannonballs ahoy! Fire!'

Pow! I kicked the football towards the hole. Bobby dived and batted it clear.

For the rest of the day, I attacked and Bobby defended his pirate ship goal. We had the best sea battle in the premiership!

Chapter 3

Next day we went to look at the harbour. Children were jumping off the wall into the sea. It made my tummy go all wobbly just looking down. The water churned away miles below. Beside me, a boy flung himself into the air, legs flying as if he was on a bicycle.

'Like pirates,' said Bobby, remembering a scene where the hero dives down to rescue a girl who has fallen from a sea wall.

'Charlie,' he said, with a special look on his face.

'No,' I said firmly. No way was I going to jump off. I hated all water, but especially dark weedy water which might be full of sharks!

'Please play pirates.' Bobby put his head on one side and smiled.

'No way,' I said, moving back from the edge. 'Ask Semi or Striker.'

'Need a girl,' Bobby explained. 'Pirates save girls.'

'Well, this girl doesn't need saving, and as I'm the only girl in this family you'll just have to play football.'

But Bobby had remembered our newest signing: Semi's girlfriend, Primrose.

He tugged her arm and explained what he wanted her to do. She peered over the sea wall, turned a bit green, and shook her head. 'Sorry, Bobby – it's too high for me.'

When his face fell she added,

'But you can rescue me when we get back to the beach.'

Bobby crumpled. He curled up on the ground and started moaning, softly at first, then louder. People gathered around. An old lady came and asked, 'Are you all right, dear?'

He warbled even louder. I hate it when that happens – people think we're being mean to him. And then there's the problem of getting him away. Mum would have shown him a yellow card, but she was down on the beach.

If we just walked away and left him everyone would think we were cruel.

We couldn't leave him, but we

couldn't get him to budge.
Wembley and Striker shrugged
hopelessly.

Suddenly, a high-pitched voice
cried, 'Help me. Oh, please help
me! I'm going to fall!'

I turned. Semi was tottering
along the sea wall, wearing
Primrose's bikini
top, a sarong,
and a pink
sun hat!

'Oh dear – oh help – I need a pirate!' he squeaked.

Bobby shot to his feet as Semi flounced into the air, skirt billowing, hat flying, saying, 'Thank goodness I remembered my clean knickers!'

Splosh! He bobbed about in the waves. Bobby scrambled onto the wall, checked everyone was watching, and shouted, 'Coming, darling!' Then without a moment's fear, he jumped.

Soon the two of them were
climbing up the harbour ladder,
Semi spraying water from his
mouth and brushing seaweed from
his eyes, said, 'Oh, thank you,
Pirate, you saved my life!'

Everyone cheered and Bobby
beamed with pride.

Chapter 4

Next day, the rain hammered on the caravan roof. I sat and read football magazines while Bobby drew skull and cross bones flags in his scrap book. The big ones stayed in bed and snored loudly.

'Let's go into town,' Mum suggested.

'Cross bones,' Bobby said.

'How about a treasure hunt?' said Dad slyly.

Soon we were sploshing through puddles, and dodging waves crashing over the sea front.

Suddenly Bobby darted off into the distance shouting, 'Pirates ahoy!'

We caught up with him in an amusement arcade called 'The Treasure Trove'. The walls were hung with fishing nets, cutlasses and pictures of pirates. Bobby stared.

In a dark corner, a bright shower of coins tumbled out of a machine.

'Treasure,' said Bobby softly, moving forward as a man scooped up his winnings.

'And me?' He tugged Dad's arm and pointed at the slot machine.

'You'll lose your pocket money,' Dad warned him.

'Please . . . ' Bobby weedled.

'You can have half.' Dad drew out some coins. 'But when it's gone, it's gone.'

Bobby pushed the pennies into the slot. Each one dropped down with a thin tinkle. Nothing came out of the flap.

Bobby studied his empty hand. He flipped the flap. No coins. His smile drooped. 'More?' he looked up at Dad.

'Nope – all gone. Let's go and explore.'

Uh oh – I could tell Bobby wasn't going anywhere. Looking around for something to distract him, I scanned the promenade.

'Hey, Bobs, come quick – rescue needed!'

Slowly, I walked towards a baby seagull. I could feel Bobby following me.

'Poor thing – she's trapped.' I tried not to frighten the tiny bird. She could hardly walk as her feet were caught in one of those plastic

things that hold cans together.
Bobby crept up from the other
side. The gull flapped in fright and
I was nervous about picking it up.
But Bobby just reached out and
very gently wrapped his hands
round the bird, cradling it against
his tummy. Once he was holding it,
the baby gull stopped struggling,
and I was able to free it from the
plastic.

'You've saved her, Bobby,' I
said.

'Pirate parrot?' He patted his
shoulder where he wanted the gull
to live.

'No, she needs her mum – you
must let her go.'

Bobby watched glumly as the
gull flew to freedom.

The sun appeared from behind
a cloud, and we stood wondering
what to do next. Then the big ones
turned up. Primrose linked arms
with Bobby and said, 'Come on,
pirate hero – let's win some
treasure.' She led the way to a
coconut shy. The walls were lined
with prizes – teddies, pandas,
penguins and . . .

'Parrots!' Bobby shouted excitedly.

Dad went first. He was way off target. Then Wembley tried. He skimmed a coconut but it wouldn't budge. Semi's ball clanged against the stand. Bobby's fell short. He sagged with disappointment. The

stallholder gave Primrose two free goes, but they were hopeless. I was the only one left. I knew just how much he wanted that parrot. But I was cross because he only wanted to be a pirate.

'Bobby,' I said, 'if I win a prize for you, will you play football?'

He nodded.

I felt the ball in my hand. Bobby put his fingers over his face and peeped out. I stared hard at the coconut. It was like a penalty – I had to see the spot – blot everything else out – imagine the ball's journey. In a kind of slow motion, I pulled my arm back, then flung, fast as a rocket.

Thwack!

The coconut teetered. And tottered. We all held our breaths. Then it wobbled off the stand, thudding to the ground.

The family cheered. Bobby ran round with aeroplane wings, like he does when we score a goal. We all trooped down to the beach with

Bobby's parrot proudly perched on his shoulder. Polly must have been the first pirate's parrot ever to play in goal – and she was a great defender!

Chapter 5

Our last day was lovely and sunny.
A tall-masted ship sailed along the
horizon, just like the ones in the
films.

'Pirates!' Bobby whooped,
jumping into his rubber dinghy.
Mum laughed as he began paddling
through the waves singing, 'Jumped
aboard a pirate ship an' the captain
said to me . . . ' The ship was just
a speck in the distance.

It was boring with no one to play with. The big ones were sunbathing, and Bobby was off chasing pirates.

I began practising keepie-uppies, one, two, three . . . I'd reached thirty-seven before the ball fell and rolled down to the water. I chased it, and heard a yell.

'Help! Help!'

At first I thought it was someone messing about – perhaps Bobby playing at being a girl in distress. But the next shout sounded real. Very real.

I looked out to sea. Bobby was still paddling towards the tall ship.

'Help!'

This time I spotted her, a small

figure, further out than Bobby, waving.

'Bobby!' I yelled. 'Look – over there!'

But he didn't hear.

My heart thumping, I ran back up the beach. I emptied Mum's bag, scrabbling through the keys and sun cream, and calling out, 'Girl – drowning, call the coastguard!'

The yellow and red cards were there, but not what I needed. Where was it? People began running towards the sea. Dad grabbed his phone. Finally, I found it: Mum's referee's whistle. I blew as loudly as I could, and at last Bobby turned. I pointed at the tiny

figure and yelled, 'Help her,
Bobby!'

Thrashing and splashing
through the waves, he paddled for
England!

All around me people were rushing into the water. Semi, Wembley and Striker are strong swimmers, but the waves at the shore were like a wall, and they couldn't get through them. The girl was being tugged away by the current. Only Bobby had a chance of reaching her. His arms pounded up and down like pistons as he battled through the choppy waters.

I felt useless. A crowd was growing, staring and pointing. No sign of a lifeboat. I had to do something. So I started trotting along the beach, keeping pace with the dinghy as it was pulled sideways. I tried to send beams of help to Bobby like we do when we watch each other play football. He was getting closer to the girl – close enough to reach out and grab her. My heart banged like a football rattle. 'Get her, Bobs,' I prayed. I glimpsed her head. Then another wave came. The dinghy was still there, but it was empty. The sea was deserted.

'Bobby,' I wailed.

Where was my brother?

Chapter 6

The boat bounced like a ghost. Nothing broke the grey surface. I stopped dead. A cry choked my throat.

Then, from the distance, a cheer went up. Smudging the tears from my face, I searched the sea. One – no, two figures were hanging onto the dinghy.

A surge of relief flooded through me, until I realised they were only clinging on, not safe inside the boat. They could be swept away at any moment. Soon the current would take them past the harbour, out to the open sea.

I knew in that instant that there was only one thing that would save them. And it was the worst thing in the whole world.

Chapter 7

Tearing off my shoes, I scrambled
onto the sea wall. The stones were
rough. The sun went behind a
cloud, and down below me, the sea
turned dark. My toes curled over
the edge and I felt sick. The drop
plunged away, and my feet froze to
the stone.

'Stop!' a voice cried.

A wave, like a giant hand,
tugged Bobby's dinghy out to sea.

'Stop!' The voice behind me called again, but squeezing my eyes shut, I launched myself into space. The sea walloped my feet, cold crashed around me, and darkness smothered me. My lungs hurt. They were bursting. I was going to drown.

Punching and splashing, I finally broke free and struck out towards the boat. 'Bobby, I'm com—'

A wave smacked me in the face. I struggled on through the treacly water. My muscles ached, but I was nearly there. I reached to grab the side when the sea yanked me back, like the elastic on a bungee jump. I was mad at that wave. My anger boiled over and my hands beat down on the sea. It wasn't going to stop me, not now. I smashed my way forward, and with one last pull I reached the dinghy and hauled myself over its side.

For a moment or two I gasped. 'Charlie,' I heard Bobby

whimper – it was too soon to rest.
I reached out and clutched his
arm, tugging him aboard. Then I
turned. A white, frightened face
stared up at me, her blue lips
trembling.

'Up you come,' I said, trying to drag her from the water. I pulled, but my strength gave way. She started slipping back. I was losing her.

But Bobby's arms were there.

'One, two, three,' he called, and together we hauled her up. As she tumbled into the boat, Bobby let out a cry of 'Pirates to the rescue!'

Chapter 8

Soon we were wrapped in blankets and whizzing across the bay in a lifeboat. Bobby chattered away to the lifeboat crew, and his eyes shone. The boat bounced over the waves and all too quickly we were met by a cheering crowd.

'Mummy! Daddy!' The little girl, called Ciara, waved at her parents who were crying and laughing at the same time.

'Thank you, thank you, thank you,' they said when they'd finished hugging her.

The lifeboat crew showed us round their station and gave Bobby and me a bag of goodies from their shop. Then they saluted and waved us on our way.

We were all exhausted as we drove home.

Dad asked, 'How did the pirates know when they'd found land?'

But Bobby was already asleep and it was Mum who said, 'They were SHORE of it!'

Bobby and I woke up with a start when the car drew up. Gran and Gramps were waiting to greet us.

'Welcome home, pirates!' said Gran.

'Did you find any treasure?' Gramps asked.

Bobby shook his head.

'Well' – Gran pointed to a pirate cake she had made – 'try over there.'

On top of the cake was a treasure trove.

Bobby lifted the lid of the little chest, and his face broke into a big grin. Inside was gold – chocolate gold!

'Are you going to play pirates now?' Gran asked when we'd finished the cake.

Bobby shook his head.

'Not pirates,' I said.

'No,' said Bobby. 'Lifeboats!'

I opened our bag and brought out a ball. It had a picture of a lifeboat on the side.

Bobby nodded, and we both said: 'Lifeboat football!'

About the Author

*Sophie Smiley was born in a Dominican
monastery – she says she had a very happy
childhood surrounded by Fra Angelicos and
Ethiopian priests! She now teaches English
and is also a staff member of Forest School
Camps, working with both the able and those
with learning difficulties. She is married and
has two children and they all live in
Cambridge.*

About the Illustrator

*Michael Foreman is one of the most talented
and popular creators of children's books today.
He has won the Kate Greenaway Medal for
illustration twice and his highly acclaimed
books are published all over the world. He is
married, has three sons and divides his time
between St Ives in Cornwall and London.*

Have you read the other
books about Bobby, Charlton,
and their football-mad family?

Bobby, Charlton and the Mountain

Bobby wants a football kit for the
Queen's visit to his school! Money-
making muddles, a beastly bully, and a
breathtaking penalty shoot-out lead to a
VERY unexpected meeting . . . !

ISBN 9781842701782 £4.99

Man of the Match

Bobby and Charlie are off to
summer camp. As soon as Bobby sees
Paul, he insists on being best friends
with him, even though Paul hides under
his parka. Of course Bobby insists on
playing football with Paul whatever
the planned activity really is. Charlie
has her work cut out to keep track of
them – and she has a big challenge
of her own, too – a relay race over
water, and she's petrified!

ISBN 9781842704202 £4.99

Team Trouble

Bobby and Charlton find their
elder brother Semi is being very
grumpy suddenly. He grunts rather
than talks, and won't play football!
What can be the matter with him?
All is revealed when Bobby follows
him out one evening, and discovers
there's a new member to the
family team: Primrose!

ISBN 9781842706848 £4.99